He Is Always With Me

Written By Laval Alsbrooks Jr.
Illustrated by FolksnFables LLC

ISBN 979-8-9876198-0-3 (Hardcover)
ISBN 979-8-9876198-1-0 (Paperback)
ISBN 979-8-9876198-2-7 (Ebook)
Library of Congress Control Number: 2023900963

Printed in USA
First Edition

To our Lord and Savior Jesus Christ.
Thank you for your love, mercy, and grace.
To my wife, Ashlee. To my family, and friends.
Thank you for always supporting me.
To my father.
Even though we grew apart before your passing, I know that we loved each other.
To the child(ren) we will have someday.
I love you and I am so proud of you.
To anyone who reads or listens to this book.
You are not alone.

"The LORD is close to all who call on him, yes, to all who call on him in truth."
(Psalms 145:18) NLT

One night Kevin was fast asleep in his bed until he was awakened by a flash of lightning that lit up the sky and a loud crash of thunder that shook his room.
"Mommy! Daddy!" He cried out.
"Please come! I'm scared!"

"Hey, how's my big guy?" His father asked as he walked into his room. With tears down his face, Kevin pointed towards the heavy rain attacking his window.
His father saw how upset he was and sat down beside him.

"There's nothing to be afraid of. It's just a little rain.
And rain is good for us because..."
Kevin hesitated but answered.
"I-It waters the plants and means prosperity."
His father smiled.

"And whenever you are afraid, you are never alone."
"I know."
"Do you remember why?"

Kevin thought for a moment
and then remembered.
"Because God is always with me."

God is with me when I'm scared.
He is with me when I'm brave.
God is with me when I potty.
And when I watch you shave.

God is with me when I eat.
And when I start my day.
He is with me when there's sun.
And when the skies are gray.

God is with me when I learn
To read and write in school.

He is with me at the beach
Or in the swimming pool.

I am happy God is with me. I believe it's true.
I am happy God is with me and He's with you too.

God is with me when I talk
To grandpa on the phone.
He is with me with my friends
Or when I'm all alone.

God is with me when I play
With Benny in the park.

God is with me when I'm wrong
Or sometimes make mistakes.
He is with me when I sleep
And when I'm wide awake.

I am happy God is with me. I believe it's true.
I am happy God is with me and He's with you too.

God is with me when I clean
And when I make my bed.

He is with me when I speak
And when I'm in my head.

He is with me when I'm sick
And when my stomach hurts.

God is with me when I dance
To my favorite song.
And when I doubt that He is near
He is right there all along.

I am happy God is with me. I believe it's true.
I am happy God is with me and He's with you too.

By the time Kevin sang the last line he had a huge smile on his face. He was no longer afraid.
His father tucked him back into bed and gave him a kiss on his forehead. As he headed towards the door, Kevin spoke.

"Daddy."
"Yes son."
"I love you."
"I love you too son."
Kevin went to bed happy because he was reminded that God Is
Always With Him... And God Is
Always With You Too.

Made in United States
Troutdale, OR
11/15/2024

24710474R00019